DOG TALES TOO:
Old and New

Written by: Roger Kluesner
& Sarvinder Naberhaus

Illustrated by: Gordon S. Roy

THIS BOOK BELONGS TO...

_____

Published by...

Ames Public Library
515 Douglas Avenue • Ames, Iowa 50010
www.amespubliclibrary.org

Library of Congress Control Number: 2014941322 ISBN: 9780985769734

Wynks would like to thank Amy, Jon, Jenny and Sigler for the production of this book.

Smyles opened his eyes from his afternoon nap.
The memories of leaving his home flooded back.

He missed his old library, people, and books.

He'd loved every corner, cranny, and nook.

Miss June packed his food dish and rug from the floor,
just like he'd seen her do one time before.

Miss June turned to Smyles, "Wanna go for a ride?"
Smyles jumped right onto the bookmobile's side.

"When making our stop, you can go play outside,
and when we return, you will have a surprise!"

While at the first stop, Smyles made a new friend.
"I'm Chester the Sheep Dog – I live at road's end."

But something was wrong, Chester wore a small frown.
"Hey, Chester," Smyles asked him, "What makes you so down?"

"My farm seems so different, not much feels like home.
New houses are standing where I used to roam."

Then Smyles heard June whistle. "It's time for goodbye."
Would Miss June soon tell him about the surprise?

He was sad to leave Chester, the new friend he'd found.
"Hey, Chester, come with us. We'll show you around!"

"Here's Brookside Park, where there's skating," Smyles said.

"Upstream from the bridge, sits fire engine Red."

"Beyond the bike trail is the new swimming pool.
On the dog days of summer, it's where kids stay cool.

We liked Brookside Park as it was before,
and now near the pool, it's loved even more."

Next on their trip was a lake by a ridge,
and town folks with fishing poles under a bridge.

"Here's Ada Hayden with busy new trails.
I walk with my friends here telling Dog Tales."

"This was an old quarry, a large gravel pit,
where I used to play and a crane used to sit."

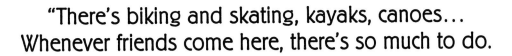

"There's biking and skating, kayaks, canoes...
Whenever friends come here, there's so much to do.

Though this end of town was so rustic before,
becoming a park, makes it loved even more."

Next Chester noticed
a stage with a shell,

a place Smyles told him
he knew very well.

"Many musicians perform on the stage.
Ames Bandshell Park just gets better with age."

"Families gather from all over town.

They listen to music. Kids play all around."

"We liked Bandshell Park as it was before,
and with the kids' playground, it's loved even more."

Rounding the corner, Smyles saw the surprise.
His library home was now double the size!

June parked and they jumped off the bookmobile's side.
Smyles raced through the crowd – "I'm home!" he cried.

Miss June cut the ribbon across the front door

and invited everyone in for a tour.

"It's my Little Theater
I've known since a pup,

And in the far corner, now what did he see?
"Look there," he told Chester, "Smyles Corner, that's me!"

"You know what," said Chester. "Your home's Old and New.
It's changed just like mine has; now I'm not so blue.

I can't herd my sheep far beyond pasture's end,
but I can still guard them and I've made a new friend."

When everyone left, and things settled back down,
then only Smyles and Miss June were around.

She placed his old food dish and rug on the floor.
Smyles loved his new library home even more.

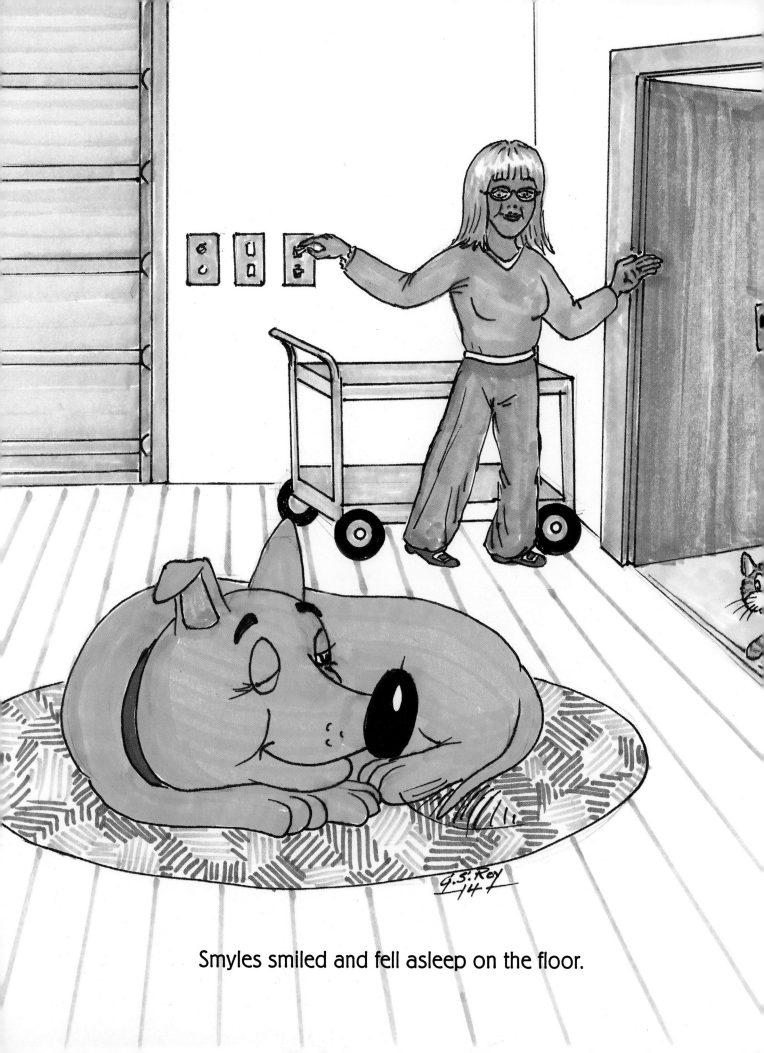

Smyles smiled and fell asleep on the floor.